THE TOWN THAT WENT SOUTH

BY CLIVE KING

Illustrated by Maurice Bartlett

PUFFIN BOOKS

PUFFIN BOOKS

Penguin Books Ltd, 27 Wrights Lane, London W8 5TZ (Publishing and Editorial)
and Harmondsworth, Middlesex, England (Distribution and Warehouse)
Viking Penguin Inc., 40 West 23rd Street, New York, New York 10010, USA
Penguin Books Australia Ltd, Ringwood, Victoria, Australia
Penguin Books Canada Ltd, 2801 John Street, Markham, Ontario, Canada L3R 1B4
Penguin Books (NZ) Ltd, 182–190 Wairau Road, Auckland 10, New Zealand

First published in the USA 1959
Published in Great Britain by
Hamish Hamilton 1969
Published in Puffin Books 1970
Reprinted 1972, 1978, 1981, 1983, 1984, 1986, 1988

Set, printed and bound in Great Britain by
Cox & Wyman Ltd, Reading
Set in Intertype Baskerville

Contents

GUNGARDEN
STREET
LION STREET
EAST
FISHMARKET
THE HIGH
EAGLE ROAD
ROPE WALK
LEVEL CROSSING

MAP OF RAMSLY
WATCHBELL STREET
TRADERS PASSAGE
MERMAID STREET
WEST STREET
UNDERCLIFF
THE STRAND QUAY
MARKET ROAD
STATION

1. Water Everywhere

GARGOYLE slipped through the shadows of the churchyard. The wind was chasing ragged clouds across the moon, the weathercock at the top of the steeple faced North-east, and the cord slapping against the flagpole on the church made a noise like an old man snipping with shears. The old ladies of Church Square, now asleep in the oak-beamed bedrooms, thought of Gargoyle as a surly, lazy cat who spent all day sitting by the fire or on sunny window-ledges. So he did, but at night, even on a wild night of March gales, he had his hunting grounds.

From the top of the town, the oldest part of Ramsly, where the oak beams looked blacker and the whitewash whiter in the moonlight, Gargoyle trotted silently down the cobbled streets, past the windows full of

shadowy fudge, home-made cakes and pottery, past the shut banks and grocers' shops in the High Street, down to the silent cinema and snack bars and along to the level-crossing. Just the other side of the railway line Gargoyle knew there were meadows with field mice and even young rabbits, and ponds with young ducklings on the banks. Gargoyle was not particular, and the old ladies of Church Square would have been horrified if they had known that the lazy rectory cat became a hunting panther on moonlit nights.

But where there should have been railway lines Gargoyle found only water. Cold, choppy water as far as he could see, and the spray blown from the tops of the waves tasted salty.

'Something wrong here,' grumbled Gargoyle to himself. 'People are always changing things. Never satisfied with things as they are. They've taken away the railway lines and put water instead.'

Gargoyle wandered off along Eagle Road to the Fishmarket, along the Undercliff to the Strand, half-way round the edge of the town. All these names meant that hundreds of years ago, before the sea had gone away from Ramsly and left marshes and flat fields for sheep to graze on, the town had been nearly an island. But Gargoyle only saw that his hunting grounds of pasture and dyke had gone, and there was nothing but salt water all round. He completed his tour of the town, past the windmill and the oldest gas-works in England and back to the railway station. The platform was now a landing-stage with waves lapping against it, but Charlie the porter, who had to meet the train with the milk and newspapers on it, was sleepily pushing a broom.

'Have you got anything to do with this?' asked Gargoyle crossly. 'What's the idea?' he grumbled. 'No railway lines, no fields! Why can't they leave things alone.'

' 'Allo, Puss!' said Charlie, who hadn't rubbed the sleep out of his eyes enough to notice how far the water went. 'Whatsa matter? Looks a bit wet, don't it? But there's been no phone call from up the line so you'll get your milk I reckon.'

Charlie didn't understand Gargoyle's language, and Gargoyle didn't understand about telephones, so he left the station in disgust and made his way back to the rectory. Dawn was only just beginning to make the sky a little lighter.

The Vicar was the second person in Ramsly to get up. He was poking about in the scullery trying to light the stove when Gargoyle scratched at the back door.

'It's gone!' complained Gargoyle loudly. 'It's all gone! You ought to do something about it.'

'What's the matter with the cat?' said the Vicar to himself. He didn't understand cat language either, though as he had no family he often carried on long conversations with Gargoyle. 'Milk's not come yet, Puss.'

'Come and see for yourself,' said Gargoyle. 'Water everywhere!' He ran a few paces towards the church, and then stopped as the Vicar did not seem to be following him. 'Don't just stand there, come and see!'

Wondering what animals would be coming to next,

the Vicar followed Gargoyle to the church, through the door to the tower, up the wooden staircase, past the works of the old clock and the bell ropes hanging in clusters, up to the dusty belfry and out on to the tower, just as the chilly gilded cherubs beat out a quarter past five with their hammers on a bleak March morning. The Vicar blinked like an owl in the weak dawn light. Instead of the miles of flat marshland, the lighthouse, the wooded hills to the North and the cliffs to the West that you could usually see from Ramsly church tower, there was now nothing but low grey clouds and a grey-green sea ending in a lead-pencil straight line all the way round the horizon.

'The whole of England gone!' said the Vicar. 'I suppose it shouldn't surprise me, but I wonder why Ramsly's spared – of all places?'

Pulling on as many bell ropes as he could reach, the Vicar was trying to wake the people of Ramsly. The jangle of bells bounced among the old red-tiled roofs and rolled down the cobbled streets, but the people of Ramsly only turned over crossly in their beds wondering why the bell ringers couldn't find a better time to practise. It was hundreds of years since the bells of Ramsly had brought the volunteers out of their beds, armed and ready to fight off raids from over the Channel. Nothing happened in Ramsly these days. Nearly exhausted but still pulling manfully after twenty minutes, the Vicar did not hear a heavy tread on the stairs.

'Oh, it's you, Vicar,' said Police-Sergeant Rock.

'What's up? You're making a lot of noise, you know.'

The Vicar let go the ropes and the bells clanged to a stop. 'It's the floods, Sergeant. Or perhaps I should say the Flood.'

'I haven't had no notification about no floods,' said the Sergeant. 'Nor I don't see what it's got to do with waking folks up out of their beauty sleep.'

'My dear fellow – ' said the Vicar. 'Just go and have a look from the tower.'

When the Sergeant came down from the tower his face was several shades less pink than it had been, in spite of the effort of getting round the narrow corners.

But even with the help of Sergeant Rock and the constables going from door to door and telling everyone what had happened, it was nearly three hours before the people of Ramsly were gathered in front of the Town Hall – at least, the people who mattered: the Mayor, the councillors and aldermen, the Fire Brigade, the Town Band – and of course the old ladies of Church Square. Gargoyle looked up at the jumble of legs. Quite a few of the trousers had flannel pyjamas underneath, he noticed. He listened to the ill-tempered voices and he could tell by the sound that many people were missing their breakfast and were not even ready to say 'Good Morning' politely, let alone discuss the End of the World, which seemed to be what all the excitement was about.

Then Gargoyle noticed that the grey early morning clouds had blown away and the sun was just beginning to shine on the front of the Town Hall. Even a March sun is better than no sun, so Gargoyle jumped on to one of the window-ledges and curled himself up. No sooner had he made himself comfortable than the sun in the sky moved steadily behind the Town Hall roof and left him in shadow. With a growl of disgust he jumped down and moved towards a patch of sunshine on the opposite pavement. That too moved on, and the sun reappeared in the bit of sky between the Town Hall and the church tower.

This was too much. Gargoyle marched on up to the Town Hall where the Mayor was still arguing with the Vicar as to who should speak first and what they were to say anyhow, and spoke as loudly and clearly in his cat voice as he could.

'The sun's got loose now. What are you going to do about that? Just take a look at it!'

And a silence fell on the people of Ramsly gathered outside the Town Hall, as they followed the gaze of the cat and saw the sun, which for as long as they could remember had risen over the marshes to the East and done its daily journey to the cliffs and wooded hills West of the town, now apparently making a swift but steady tour right round the sky, just above the tiled roofs and brick chimney-stacks.

There were two people in that gathering whom the sickening sight of the shadows swinging across the cobblestones, did not, for some reason, fill with dismay. One was Captain Voicepipe, many years retired from the Navy, and the other was Jem Shingle, once a skipper in the Ramsly Bay fishing fleet but who now made a living acting as model for the local artists, who liked the gold rings in his ears. The two old sailors looked at each other without speaking, without even thinking very much, and then nodded.

'Swingin' a bit ain't she, Cap'n Voicepipe, sir?' said Jem Shingle.

'Your worship,' said Captain Voicepipe firmly and clearly. 'In my opinion we're afloat.'

Still nobody spoke. Then from the back of the crowd came a thin, familiar voice, a voice which came from the portable radio slung from the shoulder of Brenda Roll, who was typist at the Town Hall and liked a bit of music in the lunch hour.

'Here is the news. Last night's gales caused widespread floods and damage in the South of England . . .'

Everyone listened in silence until the end.

'They don't say anything about Ramsly floating away from England,' complained the Mayor.

'I don't suppose they've noticed,' said the Vicar.

2. All at Sea

THE headquarters of the Sea Cadets was an old boat-yard down by Rock Channel where once, before the harbour silted up with mud, fleets used to ride at anchor. It was a ramshackle old building with wooden ladders and ratholes, and a sail loft full of ropes and blocks and tackles. The Sea Cadets used to meet there to learn knots and splices and Gargoyle used to catch rats.

At this moment it was the only place in the floating town where things were happening. As soon as the people of Ramsly realized they were no longer attached to the land, the seasickness began. To be the only town saved from the Flood had not surprised the Ramslyers too much; to be the only town that ever floated away to sea was too much for their stomachs. The chemists soon ran out of seasick pills and shut their doors. The

Mayor took to his bed; the Police stayed very quietly in the police station. There was nobody about in the streets. But the Sea Cadets and Captain Voicepipe had gathered in the old sail loft; there was work for them to do. And Gargoyle was there, too. Cats are never seasick, and he was curious to know what was going on.

'It's up to us now!' Captain Voicepipe was booming. 'We're going to organize things in a seamanlike manner. Don't have to worry about the engine-room fellers – got no engines! But the ship – I mean the town – has got to be steered. We've got to have a fo'c'sle party in case we need to come to anchor, look-outs on the bridge, signalmen. Plenty of work for everybody.'

Gargoyle dozed on a coil of rope.

'Steering first!' went on the Captain. 'Where are your quartermasters?'

Three small cadets stepped forward.

'Very good! Report to the wheelhouse! At the double now!'

No one moved.

'Well, what are you standin' there for?' thundered the Captain.

'Don't know where the wheelhouse is, sir,' faltered the smallest of the cadets.

'Don't know where the wheelhouse is? How long have you been on this ship – this town? Don't *know* where? ...' The Captain was suddenly silent. He thought for a minute. There wasn't a wheelhouse. There wasn't a wheel. There wasn't even a rudder. What a way to run a Navy!

'As you were!' he ordered quietly. 'Fo'c'sle party then! Can't steer – have to anchor! Fall in the fo'c'sle party!'

Still no one moved.

'Come along now! Surely you've got a fo'c'sle party. Have I got to clear away the anchor myself?'

Blank looks once again. Again the Captain began to have doubts. Was there an anchor? Could there be a cable strong enough to hold a floating town?

'Hrrumph!' growled the Captain. 'Since we're so – so short-handed we'll have the lot of you on the bridge. Grab that lot of signal flags, me lad! You, bring the charts! Telescope and binoculars, you! Fall in outside on the quarterdeck!'

They hurried down the wooden ladder on to the gravel yard they called the quarterdeck and fell in smartly in three lines.

'Into file, left turn!' barked the Captain. 'Double away smartly now! Lead on up to the bridge!'

The Sea Cadets doubled away in a smart and seamanlike manner. They hadn't a clue where the bridge was! Neither had the Captain.

But Gargoyle knew the best place for keeping an eye on things, and for catching sparrows. He scampered on ahead and led the way up to the church tower.

Squatting on the parapet, Gargoyle narrowed his eyes as he gazed at the misty horizon.

'Captain,' he remarked, 'isn't that a boat over there beyond the South Transept?'

'What's that cat doin' here?' asked Captain Voicepipe, looking towards Gargoyle.

'Ship on the starboard beam, sir!' sang out the brightest of the Sea Cadets, who had read all the right yarns and knew better than to talk about South Transepts anyhow.

The Captain swung his telescope. Sure enough, there was a small tramp steamer steering out of the mist straight for Ramsly. A stream of possible orders flashed through the Captain's mind: Alter Course to Starboard, Sound Two Blasts on the Siren, Order her to Heave To, Put a Shot Across her Bows. . . . There didn't seem to be anything the Captain of a floating town could do about a merchant vessel heading straight for his gasworks, but something had to be done quickly.

'Go and ring the church bells!' barked the Captain. 'The feller must be blind,' he muttered.

On the bridge of the *S.S. Maria Marten*, the Second Mate rubbed his eyes, rubbed them again, pinched himself, and then knocked his head deliberately against the standard compass. It was no good. Since leaving America three weeks ago they had been through a hurricane, the engines had broken down three times, the cargo had shifted and the skipper had got mumps. He knew he hadn't had enough sleep for weeks, and this wasn't the first time he had caught himself dreaming with his eyes open. But he knew, too, that there was no such thing as a floating town, with a church and church bells, gas-works and railway station in the middle of the sea. He thought if he shut his eyes and counted a hundred without actually going to sleep, it would all go away.

As Captain Voicepipe jumped about angrily on the church tower and threatened to report her to the Admiralty, the *Maria Marten* steamed straight along the east side of the town, so close as nearly to scrape the paint off her side, and even seemed to brush against the may tree which still clung to the side of Fishmarket Road where the playground used to be, before steaming straight off again into the mist.

The Second Mate didn't look back, but when the First Mate asked him some time later what he thought a dirty great thorn bush was doing tangled in the port-side boat davits he started rubbing his eyes and pinching himself again. So there had been something after all, though he must have dreamed the bit about the church bells.

Anyway, they sent off a radio signal about a dangerous piece of floating wreckage, and this was the first news to the rest of the world of the floating borough of Ramsly being sighted at sea.

After this the weather closed down even more. A white sea fog wrapped Ramsly in a cotton-wool blanket, the wind had died down, and unless you went right down to the water's edge there was only the very gentle lapping of wavelets all round the town to tell that it was surrounded by the sea. The townspeople began to feel better, and, forgetting about seasickness, got out of their beds and began to make tea (though there was still no milk). And in the near silence, something became noticeable. Ramsly was not just floating, but moving through the sea. A gentle bow wave built up at the foot of the cliff where the old tower stood, the water flowed northwards along the sides of the Strand Quay and Fishmarket Road, on opposite sides of the town, and beyond the railway station and the gas-works there was a gently boiling wake. Deep down below the surface, an undersea current was driving the floating rock on which Ramsly stood, on its voyage to no one knew where.

As Gargoyle roamed the streets that evening he saw and heard things he had never heard before. From the Jolly Smuggler tavern there actually came the sound of sea shanties; the Town Hall buzzed with excitement as the tradespeople came and went with plans for feeding and clothing the town from the stocks in the shops; in Church Square, people leaned out of windows, asked each other into drawing-rooms and chatted in large groups with neighbours they hadn't spoken to for twenty years. In the wireless shop a busy group was taking television sets to pieces and building a transmitter. Gargoyle sniffed at all this unusual activity and wandered into Jeakes's dairy. In a yard full of empty bottles, Mr Jeakes was sitting unhappily on a wire crate. Gargoyle rubbed himself against his legs.

'There ain't going to be no milk, Puss,' said Mr Jeakes. 'It's a crying shame, that's what it is.'

When daylight came next morning Ramsly floated in a grey world, in which it was difficult to say where the sea ended and the sky began. It was difficult, too, to believe that there was anything else in the world but the town, the sea and the sky. There were no letters for the postmen to deliver, no trains and no traffic came into the town, although it would have been market day if things had been normal. And though radio sets still picked up programmes from the outside world, the best electrical brains of Ramsly had still not managed to make a transmitter so that messages could be sent out.

Captain Voicepipe paced the Gun Garden as if it were a quarterdeck – twenty paces, turn round, twenty paces back again. With him paced the Mayor, who found this sort of exercise rather tiresome and wondered why the Captain couldn't go for a walk around the town. The Mayor's spaniel watched in mournful bewilderment; it wasn't his idea of a walk. Gargoyle watched, from the top of a wall. They both pricked their ears. The muffled sound of an aeroplane sounded in the cloud.

As it grew louder the Mayor and the Captain heard it, too. 'Do you think it'll spot us?' asked the Mayor doubtfully.

'They'll find us all right, with these radar gadgets,' said the Captain. 'If they're looking for us, that is.'

Suddenly the whine of the jet engine came right towards them. A small fighter plane roared out of the cloud at the level of the church steeple, banked wildly to avoid hitting it, and shot in a surprised sort of way straight up again into the cloud, leaving the golden weathercock spinning dizzily. The sound of the engine followed it, some distance behind, and could then be heard circling cautiously nearer. Out of the mist shot the plane again and, banking hard, circled right round the town just above the water in about three seconds, looped up and flipped over and circled the town the other way, so close that they could see the pilot waving and making signs at them, and then it was off again in the mist and the engine noise eventually sorted itself out and hurried off into the mist after it.

'He'll know us again the next time he meets us,' said the Mayor.

The silence of the seas returned, and the people of

Ramsly, excited for a while by having a jet pilot suddenly waving at them through their windows, began to wonder, as the hours passed, whether anyone was going to bother about them after all.

Gargoyle sat on the edge of Strand Quay, looking out over the smooth oily water. Sometimes you can see under a sea fog when you can't see over or through it. Suddenly he realized he was looking at a great grey hulk of metal, floating not far away from the town. There came the sound of pipes, bugle calls and barking loud-speakers. The mist swirled and lifted and there it was – something like a Noah's Ark in shape – an aircraft carrier, hove to a few cables' length from the quay.

Hundreds of sailors came pouring up hatchways to line the sides of the flat flight deck. A marine band appeared and struck up 'I've Come To Take You Home, Kathleen'. Then there was silence, the bugle rang out again, the flag dipped in salute and a crisp voice rang out over the water from a loud-speaker.

'Hallo Ramsly! Hallo Ramsly! *H.M.S. Incredible* calling. This is operation Noah's Ark. We shall take off your sick and aged first, and then the rest of you. Will everyone please remain calm.'

Gargoyle, sitting on the edge of the quay, twitched a whisker. He had a feeling that this buzzing beehive of steel lying over the water was not for him.

The gangway was down on *H.M.S. Incredible*; a white-painted motor launch was lowered smoothly into the water, circled smartly round to pick up a brass-covered officer at the gangway, and purred over the gentle swell towards the quay. The band played, the ship's company cheered, and Able Seaman Sippers, standing in the bows of the launch, knew he was making history as the first Naval Seaman to land on a floating town for a rescue operation. Able Seaman Sippers leapt ashore, picked up a black-and-white cat that happened to be standing right at the edge of the quay, and well aware that his words would be printed in all the newspapers, Able Seaman Sippers said:

'It's all right, Puss. The Navy's here!'

Gargoyle bit Able Seaman Sippers smartly in the right thumb and bolted up the steps to Trader's Passage, and the gallant Able Seaman's words were not, after all, printed in the newspapers.

After that, Operation Noah's Ark didn't go at all as it had been planned. While the Admiral and the Mayor first of all talked things over in the Mayor's parlour over a few drinks, and then the Mayor and Corporation went over to the ship to talk things over again, the sailors were given leave to spend their money in the teashops and souvenir shops of Ramsly, and the children of Ramsly were invited to a tea-party on board the ship and were taken up and down in the aircraft lift and allowed to work the guns and sit in the planes, and a dance was got up at the Youth Club and another one at the Dragon Hotel and at the end of it all nobody could be persuaded to leave Ramsly except the brightest of the Sea Cadets, who, years later when he was an Admiral, used to boast that he was the only man in the Navy who'd had a warship sent to his back door to ask him to join.

So the people of Ramsly decided it was fun being a floating town, though as *H.M.S. Incredible* steamed away next morning they all began to feel a little lonely again. Councillor Grouch said to the Mayor that it was all very well selling postcards and pottery to sailors but what about the water supply? And the Mayor had to admit that for some reason he hadn't been thinking about drinking-water when he was on board the *Incredible.* And Gargoyle felt happier as peace and quietness returned to the cobbled streets of Ramsly, though there was still no fresh milk.

3. Café au Lait

As Gargoyle prowled absent-mindedly about the rat-holes of Church Square that night, he was the only person in Ramsly to stay awake after the excitements of the day. The night wind was absent-minded too; mostly it blew gently from the West, and carried to Gargoyle's nose the distasteful smell of thousands of miles of salt water, but sometimes the weathercock creaked round to the South-east, and Gargoyle was disturbed by what he thought was the scent of growing things, of farms, of cows – of milk!

'Imagining things, that's what you're doing,' he grumbled to himself. 'There's nothing but this sea stuff all round.'

But the puffs of land smell kept coming, and almost without thinking Gargoyle began making his way down his usual route to his hunting grounds, down the cobbled streets, the High Street, down to where the gates of the level-crossing had been standing all day as a guard rail between the town and the open sea. And there, beyond them, instead of the hedged meadow that had always been there in the good old days, and instead of the salt waves that had suddenly taken their place, were ledges of rock covered with damp seaweed and beyond them low cliffs with what smelt like grass on their tops.

Gargoyle did not wait to be surprised. With an easy cat leap he landed on the spongy seaweed and picked his way between rock pools in the moonlight until he came to drier rock and at last to the cliff top.

From the top of a loose stone wall he picked up the familiar scents of hay-ricks and farm-yards. Lifting his feet daintily he crossed a muddy ploughed field, and then he was among the dark farm buildings, listening to the scuffle and squeak of rats and mice in holes and runways.

An owl hooted – cat-smells and sudden panics

among the mouse people told him that he was not the only hunter here. So much the better, he thought, the others can do my work for me. He settled by a likely hole in the base of a haystack and waited. Not for long – a terrified mouse came fleeing round the corner of the stack, making for the hole. Gargoyle pounced and the mouse knew no more. Gargoyle knew better than to play with his victims in the dark.

As he expected, round the stack on the track of the fleeing mouse came another cat, a grey one. Gargoyle glared at it, and growled through a mouthful of mouse. The stranger froze.

'My mouse, I believe,' said the grey cat, icily.

Gargoyle gave another smothered growl and twitched his tail.

'I have not the honour of your acquaintance, Mister Black-and-white,' spat the grey cat.

Gargoyle glared.

'Indeed I must ask you to leave this farm. This is *my* hunting ground,' said the grey cat.

Gargoyle was not one for arguing. He dropped the mouse and went for the grey cat with all teeth and claws. The struggle was short. A few wisps of grey, black-and-white fur were still floating in the moonlight air when the grey cat had fled.

Dawn was beginning to break. There came a clanking of pails from a cowshed and Gargoyle saw a woman actually putting out a bowl of milk for a group of expectant cats, among them his grey rival. Gargoyle walked confidently up to claim his share, and the grey cat and the others who seemed to look to him as their leader waited respectfully while he lapped. When he was satisfied he calmly washed his face and paws and set out for home.

The low tide had left even more of the rocks between the land and the town high and dry, though the colour of the water at the foot of the cliffs showed how deep it was along this coast on to which the floating island of Ramsly had drifted. Gargoyle scrambled back under the level-crossing gates and as he trotted along the still sleeping streets of the town he felt that after all things had turned out rather well.

It was some of the Ropewalk Street children who were next to discover the new land Ramsly had picked up. Without waiting for breakfast young Ron, Len and Brenda Boots had skipped down the street, clambered over the level-crossing gate and jumped down on to the slippery rocks. This was not so different from some of the coast that Ramsly had possessed before it broke away, though wilder and without a caravan camp in sight, but they soon got tired of looking in rock pools and decided to see what was on the other side of the cliffs. Ron, the eldest, got to the top first, and the other two still had some way to go when they saw him poised on the skyline on a wall of loose stones. Suddenly he jumped back on to the grassy slope and seemed to be making signs for them to be quiet and stay where they were.

'What's up, Ron? We're coming,' called Len, pretending not to understand. If there was something interesting to see he wasn't going to be put off seeing it.

Ron's signals became even more urgent, and he came

sliding down the slope on the seat of his trousers with a cross expression on his face.

'Keep quiet, I tell you,' he hissed. 'Don't let him hear you.'

'Don't let who hear us?' asked Brenda. 'I don't believe you've seen anyone. Who is it, the Sheriff of Nottingham?' Brenda was used to Ron's tricks and inventions, and was quite prepared to hear a description of anything from a Red Indian war party to a Martian with a green face and a space helmet.

'There's a man there in a blue dress driving a plough with two cows,' said Ron shortly.

The other two thought about this for a while in silence. This was something new, and they suspected that Ron was breaking the rules.

'Go on!' said Len. 'That's just soppy. Let's play we're smugglers and you've just seen the customs men.'

'I'm not playing anything!' said Ron fiercely. 'I told you what I've seen. Go and see for yourself if you don't believe me. But don't let *him* see *you* or we're done for.'

He spoke as if he were telling the truth, though you never could tell with Ron, and Brenda, who was only seven, began to feel unhappy. It wouldn't have been too bad if they had met a real Indian chief or even a real Martian – everybody knew what was the right thing to do with them – but a man in a blue dress driving a plough with two cows might do anything. She wasn't sure she even wanted to look, but the two boys had started to crawl on their stomachs up the slope towards the stone wall, so she followed, her heart beating

loudly. They reached the top and very cautiously and quietly peeped over the wall.

On the other side was a field of brown earth sloping down to a whitewashed farm, and moving across it were two great white beasts with horns, harnessed to a queer old-fashioned plough guided by a man with long moustaches, a long blue smock, black trousers and wooden shoes.

As the three of them stared with open mouths, Len

put his weight too heavily on one of the loose stones on the top of the wall and it fell to the ground with a clatter. The man in the blue smock looked round, but the children had already bobbed down behind the wall and were sliding breathlessly down the slope with a funny feeling in their insides that wasn't only because they'd had no breakfast. Hardly daring to look round to see if they were being followed, they scrambled over the cliff edge and made their way over the rocks to where Ramsly lay against the jagged coast like a great stranded battle-ship.

Of course by the time they got back, most of the people of Ramsly had wakened up to the fact that they had struck land again, but though all the landward windows were full of people, nobody could make anything of the desolate coast and the few distant buildings that were in sight. And of course the children were bombarded with questions as to where they had been, what they had been up to, what did they mean by going off like that without asking and did they think they were going to get any breakfast now? Ron, knowing the way of grown-ups, wouldn't say anything except that he'd seen a man and some cows, but when Brenda burst into tears and told the full story of the cows pulling the plough and the man in the blue dress and wooden shoes, the grown-ups for some reason said, Poor little thing, she's over-excited, and they blamed the boys for leading her astray and filling her head with ideas.

But though nobody except Gargoyle and the three children had yet been ashore to explore this unknown land, the men of Ramsly had not been wasting their time. Colonel Sackem had been retired from the Army for quite a long time, but though he supposed that it was all right for Captain Voicepipe to take command when the town was actually at sea, he felt that when it came to organizing a landing party, it was time *he* did some organizing. He had routed out what was left of his battledress, which he had worn for digging the garden for some years now, and gathered together a collection of volunteers, all of whom he insisted should wear uniforms. As he explained, you couldn't be shot as a spy so long as you were wearing uniform. There turned out to be more volunteers than he expected, so eventually he had to pick one of the police-sergeants, three firemen (complete with brass helmets), a member of the Town Band who had brought a bugle, and two Boy Scouts who turned out to be the only people in the town who were really capable of sending semaphore signals if it was necessary.

Gargoyle, up on the church tower again in his usual hopeful search for sparrows, looked down curiously on the scene as the little party set off on their reconnaissance. The first obstacle was the gap between the level-crossing gates and the rocks, which Gargoyle had taken in a cat leap in the dark and the children had scrambled across without thinking. The Colonel insisted that a proper bridge should be constructed before they could even begin, and also to make sure of their line of retreat. After all he wasn't as young as he used to be, and the Police-Sergeant wasn't as light as he used to be. By this time most of the population of Ramsly was down by the level-crossing, all full of suggestions and eager to help, and the scouts started lashing staves together and the men from the builder's yard came out with planks and scaffolding, and everybody who had a ladder brought it along. Eventually the thing which seemed to fit best was a machine for loading hay on to haystacks which was in the repair yard. The mechanic was very eager to set the engine working but the Colonel said that a bridge was one thing but a moving staircase was just spoiling the troops.

Gargoyle was still watching as, after much of the morning had gone, the patrol was led by the Colonel on to the rocks. Apart from a few soaked trouser legs as booted feet slipped into rock pools, there were no casualties in the first part of the landing. Slowly they could be seen mounting the grassy slope, the sunlight glinting on the brass helmets of the firemen. And only then did the watchers from the town see that on the skyline there were more figures waiting for them, trim uniformed figures in peaked pillbox caps, wearing cloaks, and armed with rifles.

The two little armies stood strung out against the blue sky. It was much too far away for anybody to hear what was being said but it was easy to see what was happening. First there were threatening movements from the rifles of the strange figures, and the watchers knew that except for a policeman's club, some firemen's axes and scout staves, the Ramsly party was not armed. But they held their ground, the Colonel standing very stiffly in front of them. Then the short-cloaked leader advanced and addressed the Colonel, with much waving of hands and shaking of head. The Colonel pointed briefly at the stranded town and out to sea, and the waving and head-shaking of the other increased. There seemed to be some sort of conference as the Ramsly party put their heads together and then, just as some of the more excitable watchers from the town, including Ron Boots, were betting that there was going to be a real battle, it seemed that the Colonel had tamely gone over to the enemy and marched off with them over the skyline, while the rest of his party slowly retreated down the slope and over the rocks.

The Ramsly crowd was in quite an ugly mood as the Police-Sergeant led the way back over the bridge to town.

'Ought to be ashamed of yourselves, you men!' called old Mrs Guffle. 'Lettin' the poor old Colonel get took pris'ner by the enemy! It's a wonder you dare come back to us!' And Ron Boots shrilled from the back of the crowd: 'Go on, what about a fight?'

Sergeant Rock stood on his dignity.

'All right, all right, you can just listen here a bit,' he said as soon as there was a bit of quiet. 'Colonel Sackem asked me to say that the intentions of the natives appears to be friendly. This here's France, not the cannibal islands. He's gone into the nearest town to see the authorities and in the meanwhile nobody's to leave the town.'

There was a babble of voices as everybody spoke at once.

'Parlay voo!' 'Don't trust them foreigners ...' 'Been on a day trip to Boolown myself, they're all right really.' 'Anywheres near Armenteers, are we, Sarge?'

But once again it was Gargoyle, who, disgusted with all the talk and thinking that there might be milk for lunch as well as breakfast in this brave new world, drew all eyes to himself by trotting calmly over the gangway under the eyes of the Sergeant.

'Here, where are *you* going, Puss?' said the Sergeant.

'Wants a drink of milk, I reckon,' said old Mrs Guffle. '*And* nobody ain't going to stop him.'

'That's right,' came a voice from the crowd. 'Who says we can't go ashore? Can't do no harm.'

The Sergeant paused to think this over. He looked at the Mayor, who was at the back of the crowd, feeling rather out of things. The Mayor said nothing. Neither of them could think of any law which said that the citizens of Ramsly were not to go outside their town, but they both thought it couldn't be as easy to go from England to France as just walking over a bridge. The crowd looked at the Mayor. The Mayor cleared his throat.

'Well, as far as I know it's the first time an English borough has crossed the Channel. If you want to go ashore, there doesn't seem to be anything to stop you.' And he went back to the Mayor's parlour.

The things that happened in and around Ramsly during the next day or two meant nothing to Gargoyle. He found his farm again and made the most of what milk was going there, and was not particularly surprised to meet Mrs Guffle arguing with the farmer's wife over a basket of fresh eggs. Just round the headland he discovered a little French town with cobbled streets, not so much different from Ramsly, and was not surprised to hear the voice of Colonel Sackem talking about the last-war-but-one with the French Maire, who was also an old soldier. But what interested Gargoyle were the butchers' shops, with lots of scraps for cats. On his way back he met the Boots children riding back to the farm on the two white plough oxen, which they thought was much more fun than a tractor. He didn't particularly notice when next day men started putting up barbed wire along the French shore to stop the Ramslyers landing, and then put a gate with a frontier post and guards in it to let them through in the proper manner. Gargoyle slipped through the wire anyhow. The coming of a British warship to stand by three miles offshore meant nothing to Gargoyle, nor did the flotilla of French destroyers steaming busily up and down. A line of big army guns drawn up on the skyline overlooking the town interested him mildly, and the next thing was a helicopter hovering over Church Square, with a man in a black hat and coat, striped trousers and polished shoes, carrying a leather brief-case, coming down out of it on the end of a string.

Once again the people of Ramsly gathered outside the Town Hall. The man in striped trousers made a long speech, finishing with these words:

'It's really quite simple. The French want Ramsly to become part of France. Of course we want to stay British. I shall see to it that your homes are protected to the last British oak beam. Unfortunately that means that all the people of Ramsly must be taken off so that the troops can move in. You can trust us to look after you.'

The helicopter was hovering overhead again and the string came dangling down. The man in the striped trousers noticed a cat sitting on the Town Hall steps.

'You're coming with me, aren't you, Pussy?' he said smiling at a man with a camera.

Gargoyle bit him smartly in the right thumb as he bent to pick him up, and bolted up the steps to the Mayor's parlour.

That evening there was no singing in the Jolly Smuggler. At a time when most of the respectable citizens had gone sadly to bed, wondering if it was their last night in their old homes, Gargoyle wandered into the inn, attracted by a feeling of bristly defiance which it seemed to be giving off. Sure enough, there was a group of bearded artists and poets drinking in moody silence.

There came a knock on the door, for which the group seemed to have been waiting, and in came Sergeant Rock.

'What's going on here?' asked the Sergeant. 'It's long past closing time.'

'Have a drink, Sergeant,' said Percy Bramble, the poet. 'Landlord, a goblet of red wine for the policeman.'

The landlord's face appeared sheepishly from behind the bar.

'Come on now, Mr Bogle,' chided the Sergeant. 'You know it's well past closing time.'

'Who says it is?' growled a large bearded artist from behind a pipe in the corner.

'The law says it is, which you know very well, Mr Forester.'

'Ah, but which law?' put in Buddley-Salterton the playwright. 'French law says you can have a drink whenever you like. And we're quite a long way away from England now.'

The Sergeant pondered for a moment, then his jaw became even more rock-like than ever.

'Mr Bogle,' he said to the landlord, 'I'm surprised at you. *And* I don't care what heathen customs go on on the continent, what's right's right, and there's no drinking after ten-thirty. *Or* there'll be trouble.'

'Just what I told these gentlemen, Sergeant. Sorry gents all, time *if* you please!' And the landlord came out from the bar in a fluster and started collecting up glasses, some only half empty.

Percy Bramble bristled with indignation. 'What a country,' he said. 'It's this sort of thing that makes you want to – to Walk Out Into the Night.'

And out into the night he walked, followed by a bearded, pipe-smoking crew. And out into the storm it was too, for the wind was now blowing wildly from the East again, and spatters of rain blew in at the door as they walked out. Gargoyle watched them go regretfully because he rather liked these hairy men, and felt that he wouldn't be seeing them again. But he could come and go for his drinks of milk whenever he felt like it, so he did not feel he had to go with them.

But Gargoyle was wrong. When his midnight restlessness came upon him again and he set out for the mainland, something told him to stop at the bridge. The tide was high and sea water was swirling and sucking in the gully between the town and the land. And as Gargoyle paused in doubt the bridge creaked and groaned, and then toppled into the water foaming over the rocks. Something seemed to be pushing the rocks and cliffs beyond further and further away into the darkness. But even Gargoyle knew what was happening this time. Ramsly was putting to sea again.

4. The Warm South

THERE were two terrible days and nights of storm at sea. There was a time when the whole town really did take on a heaving, pitching motion, the church bells rang themselves and, in the houses, those most homely and secure things, the mantelpieces over the hearths, were no longer safe places to keep porcelain vases or souvenirs of Margate. But when the storm had done its worst, the old houses of Ramsly were still standing and only a few rather nasty little new sheds by the Strand had been carried away. And the floating town came out into a region of warm breezes, blue sky and sparkling clear water, and settled down into its new life as if in a dream.

Anyone could tell that the town was moving South. The creepers that used to struggle a few inches a year up the old brick walls of Watchbell Street began to spread over the eaves and clamber up the chimneys, and the air was full of their scent. The prickly pear that old Mrs Cosset had kept for years in a pot on her window-sill was knocked into the back yard one day and smashed into pieces, and every little piece took root in the cobbles so that before long she had a job to get to her dustbin. Gargoyle, and the old men who sat in the sun whenever they could, found to their surprise that they were now choosing the shade instead.

One day Miss Holly of Ye Olde Oake Beame Café was seen putting her tables and chairs out on the pavement and, though people were a bit shocked at first, they soon got used to the idea and would sit for hours under the awning over their cups of tea. Worse things than that happened. More and more people were suspected of spending the afternoons in, or rather on, their beds. The Old Wives' Guild were particularly upset about the possibility of some of their members getting this dreadful habit, and organized daily knitting and sewing parties to keep themselves busy during the warm afternoons. They were even more upset when old Mrs Guffle, one of their staunchest members, suddenly exclaimed half-way through a particularly sleepy meeting: 'I don't know why we want to waste our time making *more* clothes, I'm sure. I'm going home to take a few things off.'

It was all right for Ron and Len and Brenda and all the boys and girls of Ramsly, who had done the obvious thing and got hold of all the fishing-rods and lines they could lay their hands on, and now spent all day strung out round the edge of the town pulling in

fish almost as fast as they could sell them. But the Mayor and the Councillors and the shopkeepers went around with long faces in spite of the summery weather wondering – well, wondering what to do with themselves, with no farmers or tourists coming to spend money in the town.

Of course that side of things worked itself out very easily. All the world now knew about the floating town, and whenever it was sighted by a cruising liner it would come alongside, and rich tourists would pour into the cobbled streets, eager to buy anything with the label, 'Made in Ramsly, the Sea-Borne Borough'. Anyone who could make a pot, weave a skirt or draw a picture of Mermaid Street was making a fortune, the antique shops were soon empty and had to make urgent orders for fresh supplies by cargo vessel, and there were enough dollars and other strange money circulating round the town to keep all the banks busy.

Gargoyle was quite happy with all the fish he liked, though he still missed his fresh milk. It was about the only thing that nobody had thought of a way of organizing. Banana boats, refrigerator ships full of meat, oil tankers and tramp steamers with mixed cargoes of anything from breakfast foods to plastic toys all came alongside the Strand Quay and asked if there was anything they could deliver today. And in between the visits of ships there really didn't seem to be much that needed doing except basking in the sunshine.

One afternoon the only person who was not asleep was Captain Voicepipe, who was on top of the church tower with his telescope. He had long ago realized that

Ramsly was not a ship that could be steered or anchored, but he was never comfortable if he thought that there was nobody at all keeping a lookout. As he propped his telescope against the parapet and looked through it, he found it very difficult to keep awake on this hot and sticky afternoon. Suddenly he shook himself, took his eye from the glass and blinked.

'Dreamin' on watch, Voicepipe,' he told himself. 'Won't do!' Then he rubbed his eyes and took another careful look through the telescope to eastward.

He hadn't been dreaming. There, through the heat haze, appeared a baked brown coastline, with white buildings, and he thought he could make out rounded domes and tall spiked towers.

'Land ho!' shouted Captain Voicepipe from the top of the church tower, but most of Ramsly slept on in its afternoon siesta. Gargoyle, who had been asleep in the coolest shadow of the church walls, pricked his ears, got up and made for the belfry steps. As he got out on to the tower the Captain was squinting through a sextant at the sun. Then, ignoring Gargoyle, he did a lot of sums on the backs of envelopes, with a great deal of crossing out and head scratching.

'If anyone's interested,' said the Captain to the cat at last, 'we seem to be approaching the coast of the Kingdom of Tarboosh. Probably be more trouble. If you'll kindly keep a lookout, Number One, I'll clear lower deck myself.' And he disappeared down the ladder.

Gargoyle kept a lookout as the distant shore loomed nearer and nearer, and the details of square whitewashed houses, domed mosques and tall minarets became clearer. Now he could see crowds of people pouring on to the waterfront of the strange town and even at this distance he could see the excited state they were in. As the afternoon went on, and the floating town slowly approached the shore, the angry buzz of a great crowd could be heard above the wash of the waves.

Like a sphinx, like the stone gargoyles on the church, from which he had got his name, Gargoyle stared down from the tower on the excited human crowd. On the West Cliff he could see the Mayor, Captain Voicepipe and Colonel Sackem. Even they seemed to be affected by the waves of hate from over the water; he even saw the Colonel shake his fist. Gargoyle trotted lazily down to join them.

'If we just had a battalion of Guards, now . . .' the Colonel was saying.

'A small detachment of Marines would do it . . .' the Captain was muttering.

'Well, gentlemen, we haven't got either,' said the Mayor. 'But we've got to do *something*. We're really in for trouble this time.'

They anxiously watched the narrowing gap between Strand Quay and the crowded waterfront of Tarboosh.

'Always got to *do* something,' exclaimed Gargoyle contemptuously in cat language. '*I* think it's tea-time,' and he turned his back on them and slipped up the steps of the Hope Anchor hotel to see what he could pick up.

The Mayor, the Captain and the Colonel looked at him. Then they looked at each other. Quietly they moved among the crowds of Ramslyers waiting in suspense along the West side of the town. Quietly the people of Ramsly went home to tea. By the time the Strand Quay came with a scrunch against the pebble beach of Tarboosh, there was no one about in the streets of Ramsly.

The people of Tarboosh swarmed across the beach and into the cobbled streets, not in a wild mob, but rather like a ragged army in columns. Oddly enough the first column seemed to be made up of the youngest school-children, dressed in short smocks. After them came the older students, wearing anything from bright flapping American shirts to long striped gowns. Last came a long column of men, some with baggy trousers and round red hats, some with long robes, some with light blue shop suits. All seemed to be very angry; at places along the column there were leaders walking backwards, shouting strings of angry words over and over again, to which the followers replied with harsh sounds in chorus. Here and there were banners with strange curly writing, the paint they were written in still wet, and even one or two in English, saying things like: 'GO TO HOME BRITISH PEOPLE.'

The noisy crowd, headed by the school-children shouting in shrill chorus, surged up into the High Street, up and down the cobbled streets, along the High Street, up and down the cobbled streets, the old buildings ringing with the strange clamour of voices.

They realized that they were now going round in

circles. Also that nobody seemed to be taking any notice of them. The columns began to break up, the chanting began to die down. Silent, rather puzzled groups of Tarbooshis began to take an interest in their surroundings, peering through latticed windows and over open half-doors at the inhabitants of this strange town. They gazed with open mouths at groups of prim English ladies sitting round tables pouring tea from silver teapots. The old ladies of Church Square were accustomed to being stared at by trippers, and took no notice. Tarbooshis retreated in alarm from fierce little yapping dogs in doorways – they were not used to houses owned by dogs. Plucking up courage, Tarbooshis swaggered into oak-beamed teashops, where cold waitresses looked through them and left them sitting unhappily over plates of scones and bread-and-butter. Remembering films they had seen, dark-eyed young men in light blue suits and flowery shirts walked into hotels and grandly ordered whiskies-and-sodas, and were told they would have to wait until six o'clock.

A chill seemed to come over the hot blood of the people of Tarboosh. Their leaders had told them that the wicked people of Ramsly had come to take over their country and make slaves of them, but this strange floating town seemed to be under some cold magic spell itself, like something in their old Arabian tales. As the sun dipped towards the western sea and the shadows gathered around the old church with its windows full of mysterious pictures, so different from their bare and simple mosques, the groups who had been sitting about the churchyard eating peeled thistles began to feel the fear of the unknown. The shaven-headed school-children started to whimper and ask to go home. By nightfall at seven o'clock the people of Tarboosh had folded up their banners and crept silently away.

With them had gone Gargoyle. He had seen goats on the hills of the mainland and thought that that probably meant goats' milk. Out at the back of the town he came upon black tents pitched in the sand and there under the bright stars was a woman in a black veil putting a bowl of milk on the ground.

'These people look after cats too,' thought Gargoyle, but when a white horse came up and started drinking the milk he was quite amazed. However, the horse did not seem to mind sharing the bowl, so Gargoyle did quite well.

Morning calm lay over the twin towns of Ramsly-

Tarboosh, but Gargoyle, who liked to stay calm when other people were excited, now felt restless.

He wandered along from the vicarage to Ye Olde Oake Beame Café. Though it was only half past ten in the morning, it was full of Tarbooshi gentlemen smoking hubble-bubble pipes, playing backgammon, and drinking little cups of strong black coffee. A few of the old ladies of Church Square were there too, drinking big cups of weak milky coffee. Old Miss Holly poured Gargoyle a saucer of milk, but Gargoyle sniffed at it, waved his tail and passed on.

'There's a funny cat,' said Miss Holly. 'Don't know what's got into him this morning.'

Gargoyle trotted down the High Street. Outside Dr Hartshorn's surgery a long line of patient Tarbooshis sat on the pavement in the sun, waiting for the magic prick of the needle. He wandered into Miss Botany's shoeshop, but Miss Botany was busy selling a pair of shoes to a desert tribesman.

'It says *four pounds* on the *ticket*,' Miss Botany was saying very loudly and clearly. 'What's the use of saying you'll give me two?'

Gargoyle crossed over from the Strand to the markets of Tarboosh. Mrs Guffle and other Ramsly housewives were buying lengths of striped native cloth to make curtains.

'Go on with you!' Mrs Guffle was saying. 'Four pounds a yard for that skimpy stuff! Ought to be ashamed of yourself you ought!'

Gargoyle went down some stone steps from the market to an underground room full of steam. There Captain Voicepipe and Colonel Sackem were lying on stone slabs wearing nothing but small towels, and being beaten by a big black man. Oddly enough they seemed to be enjoying it. Gargoyle stood at the entrance to the Turkish bath in amazement. It meant nothing to him, though he did have the very faintest idea today that it would be nice to get out of his fur for once and get rid of this restless itch that was unsettling him.

Gargoyle slipped into the King's palace, passed along cool tiled passages, through courts with fountains playing, and into the Council Chamber. There, on opposite sides of a chessboard, sat the King, in white robes and gold-bound head-dress, and the Mayor of Ramsly, in his heavy robe of office with a pyjama suit underneath, losing his twenty-eighth game of chess and drinking his eighty-fourth cup of coffee. Neither spoke a word, but again, both seemed happy.

Gargoyle went up the steep streets at the back of the town, keeping out of the way of the donkeys and mules laden with melons or dates, and made for the camp of the desert tribe, where he knew he could have his choice of milk from camel, ewe or goat. Under the palm trees by a spring of water sat the silent old men of the desert; with them sat Jem Shingle and the silent old men of Ramsly. Grooming the gentle Arab ponies, or riding them bareback and without bits across the sands, were Brenda Boots and all the little girls of Ramsly who had ever dreamed of riding milk-white steeds across the desert, while the sheiks looked on in amazement at the boldness of the little English girls. Where the spring water gushed into a pool under the rock there could be seen the sunburnt bodies of the young boys, splashing and swimming, and you had to

look carefully to see that, if they were only a little bit less sunburnt, they were probably Ramsly children.

Under a rock, a shepherd boy played a thin wandering tune on a pipe.

It seemed to Gargoyle, as it seemed to many of the people of Ramsly when they didn't stop to think, that the town had reached a very pleasant end to its journey, and that time could pass swiftly and happily here forever. And yet Gargoyle felt restless. It was a new kind of restlessness, that seemed to live at the ends of each one of his hairs, as if he bristled with electric sparks. The day was getting hotter, and a particularly hot dry wind was blowing from the desert. Towards the East the sky began to look yellowish, and even the sun became dimmer. The people of the tribe muttered uneasily and moved back to the tents, the tethered camels lay down with their backs to the wind. Now the wind became stronger, and away over the desert was a great wall of flying dust and blown sand. The sandstorm was coming.

Gargoyle could have gone into the tents with everybody else, but his one idea was to get home. He felt that surely the streets of Ramsly would be free from this gritty wind, like the breath from an open oven. Blown like a bundle of rags before the storm, he ran down towards the town, was bowled around windy corners and pinned against walls by the force of the wind. From the higher streets of the town he could see men with their faces wrapped in cloths battling to tie Ramsly to the shore with great mooring-ropes, but even as he watched, the ropes drew taut as bowstrings, snapped, and flew back like elastic bands. A foaming stretch of sea began to open between the shore and Ramsly's Strand Quay as Gargoyle hurried desper-

ately through the dusty streets, though already it seemed too late. When he reached the seashore, he could hardly see the houses of Ramsly beyond the driving spray and sand. He was left behind.

And then down from the desert, over the palace, through the main square and on to the waterfront raced a gigantic dust devil, a great spinning pillar of dust, sand and litter rising high into the air. Picked up like any other scrap of rubbish, Gargoyle felt himself flying round and round through the air, above the shore, above the hissing sea and then falling, falling, towards the waves.

He landed with a bump on a sloping surface, and there he was on Ramsly church roof, while as far as he could see to eastward against the stinging sand, the coast of Africa drew farther and farther away.

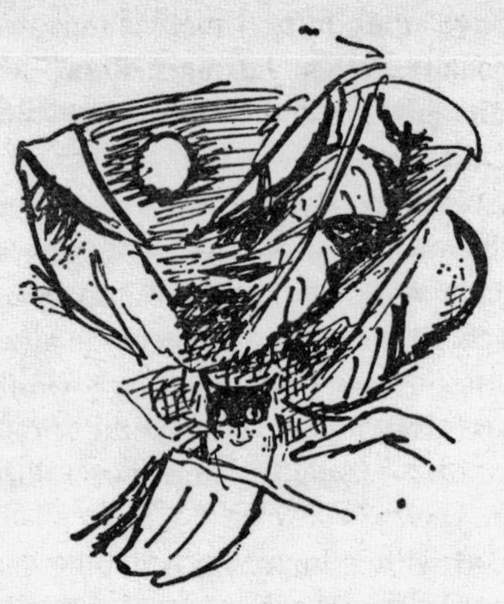

5. Black-and-White

GARGOYLE was sleeping stretched out on the stone hearth of Miss Fitzbuller's old house in Church Square. Of course there hadn't been a fire there for a long time – Gargoyle chose it as the coolest place he knew. The people of Ramsly were now beginning to find that the sun was an enemy, to be shut out of their houses by drawn curtains and closed windows. There still seemed to be a little English frost and damp stored in the stones of the oldest houses to fight the tropical heat, and people were retreating to cellars and old damp kitchens as the pleasantest places to live.

But Gargoyle's midday doze was disturbed by a burning feeling, first at the end of his tail, then creeping along his back till his whole body was drenched in heat. He woke up to find himself in a pool of sunshine – the sun was shining straight down the wide old-fashioned chimney on to the hearthstone. Ramsly was nearing the Equator.

Gargoyle got up, flicking his ears angrily. If he couldn't escape the sun, perhaps he could get some air on the church tower. He went out across the churchyard, through the palms and strange creepers that were now sprouting there, and languidly climbed the belfry steps. There was nobody on the church tower. Captain Voicepipe was still enjoying his Turkish baths in Tarboosh, with a lot of Ramsly's other old men, and the children were still playing among the tents of the desert tribe. And even further away the artists and the poets were enjoying the wines of France. What was left of Ramsly's population dozed in shuttered rooms in the heavy midday heat, and the old town floated like a dream on a glassy sea.

But through the heat haze Gargoyle saw without surprise Ramsly's third landfall, a line of low jungle stretching along the horizon. Slowly the town drifted towards the shore and then, while still some way off, seemed to stop moving. All that afternoon Gargoyle watched the land for signs of life and one by one the townspeople came out of their houses and saw the silent line of vegetation, but nothing seemed to happen. Gargoyle sat on, watching, with the patience he had learnt at a thousand mouseholes.

And then, just as the sun began to redden and sink towards the oily sea, round a headland shot a long low canoe, paddled by six black men. They stopped paddling and froze as they came in sight of the town, then after putting their heads together, paddled off in perfect time, making a wide circle round the town. Gargoyle walked round the parapet of the tower and watched them against the red wash of sunset, against the darkening mysterious jungle, and as they shot off again at speed round the coast.

Down in the streets of the town people looked at each other anxiously, and muttered:

'Natives!'

'Savages!'

'*Cannibals!*'

The sun suddenly fell behind the rim of the sea and vanished with a green flash, and there was darkness over the town of Ramsly, and the becalmed water, and the silent jungle.

But the jungle was not silent for long. Over the water came the voices of a million insects, like the sizzling of countless frying-pans, then the cries of unknown animals. And then the drums. Excited, chattering, news-carrying drums, telling the strange tale of the stranded town to all the people of the jungle. And dancing, throbbing drums from villages where people were sitting up around their fires. All night long they went on, and there was not much sleep in the anxious town of Ramsly. But Ramsly was ready for the next day when it came.

It was the High Street people who got things organized this time. Everybody knew the rules for dealing with hostile natives. All the beads from the novelty shops, all the mirrors and pocket-knives from the hardware shops, and the gayest lengths of cloth from the drapers were collected together, and everyone who had a glass eye, or false teeth, or a wig, was ordered to stand by. It was well known that the best way to impress a native was by something like that.

Early next morning the sight they expected and feared was seen. A fleet of long low canoes, with twenty black paddlers each, appeared round the coast. On the quay, sweating already in their best suits, stood the Town Clerk, the Postmaster, the Bus Company Inspector, the Electricity Manager, and all the shopkeepers with their piles of beads, cloth, pen-knives and mirrors at their feet.

The leading canoe came smartly alongside the quay and out of it stepped in a dignified manner a tall, handsome black man dressed in a bright cotton robe.

There was silence as the Town Clerk tried to remember what he had to say. They had all agreed last night that he would begin by saying: 'White man lib for peace palaver alonga black man. White man along him too much plastic beads, crease-resisting linen . . .' or something like that, but he couldn't remember a word. What he said was:

'Er. . . . Good morning!'

The shopkeepers advanced holding out their gifts, feeling rather foolish. A broad, jolly grin spread over the face of the African.

'Good morning, gentlemen! Thank you for your gifts. I appreciate the spirit in which they are offered. But they are not what we have come for.'

'Oh. What can we do for you then, Mr Er . . . ?'

asked the Town Clerk, looking anxiously at the strong white teeth and the shining black muscles in all the boats.

'I am the Prime Minister. I will tell you shortly what we want. We want Town Clerks – '

The Town Clerk turned pale.

'We want Postmasters – '

A cold trickle ran down the Postmaster's spine.

'We want Bus Inspectors – '

The Bus Inspector felt weak at the knees.

'We want Electricity Managers.'

The Electricity Manager's mouth went dry. One thought was in the mind of each one of them: *cannibals*. Each of them saw the same vision: all four in a big black pot, with a fire underneath, and naked savages dancing round them.

The African's eye fell on a black-and-white cat sitting on a heap of cloth. An even jollier grin spread over his face.

'Oh yes, we want cats too!'

This, thought all the people of Ramsly gathered on the quay, is where that cat bites the African, and then we'll *all* be killed and eaten.

The African turned to Gargoyle and bowed politely.

'Mister Cat,' he said gravely. 'As Prime Minister of this country, I have the honour to offer you the appointment of Chief Rodent Destroyer. We have many rats. We also have many rates, ha ha, and letters and buses and electric lights in our new country. We are not yet sure how to manage them. If you gentlemen,' he turned to the officials, 'are willing to

come with me, I will make you Secretaries of the Ministries of Works, Communications, Transport and Power.'

The officials gaped at each other. Which was true – their vision of naked savages or this talk full of long political words? They looked at Gargoyle.

Gargoyle walked sedately across the quay and jumped into the Prime Minister's canoe.

*

In the city Gargoyle was already tired of his job. It was all right for the Town Clerk, the Postmaster, the Bus Inspector and the Electricity Manager – they were happy at their big desks in their brand-new concrete buildings, telling people how to collect taxes, sort letters, issue tickets and read meters. There were certainly plenty of rats to catch too, but it was the jungle that called to Gargoyle. He thought it must be something like the meadow that used to be on the other side of the railway track, only more so. As night fell he set out along the new avenue lined with palm trees, that turned into a narrow motor road, that turned into a track for bullock carts, and finished up as a jungle path.

Gargoyle felt he was an animal again, indeed more

of an animal than he had ever been. In the English meadows there had been green smells of growing grass and weeds, and the night scents of wild flowers, and smells of damp earth and of rotting wood and leaves round the edges of the ponds. Here the smell of growing things, rotting things, damp soil and heavy sweet blossoms, was like a rich thick soup. And mixed with it, instead of the faint scents of English mouse and bird, were great wafts of fierce animal smell that made the fur on Gargoyle's back and tail prickle and stand on end. His ears, used to keeping alert for the feeblest squeak and scuffle, were almost deafened by the singing of insects, the chanting of frogs and the growls, hoots, chatters and roars from creatures of which Gargoyle couldn't tell bird from beast.

He began to sort out the smells now. One was a smallish, juicy kind of smell that must belong to a young animal worth eating. Gargoyle began to stalk, concentrating on hunting this thing down. But at the back of his mind there was a worry: he was aware of a very different kind of smell, a fierce cat smell, that made him think there was a rival somewhere around.

In a clearing of the jungle, where the moonlight shone more strongly, Gargoyle sighted his quarry, a fluffy young creature cowering on the ground. He did not know what it was. It was a good bit bigger than a field mouse but he thought he could deal with it. He crept through the grass, his tail twitching, ready to spring.

He sprang, but as he sprang, another large cat-like animal sprang from the other side of the glade. Both of them did their best to stop in mid-air, and came down facing each other and glaring.

'Mine!' snarled the leopard. 'Get out!' he spat. 'Who do you think *you* are?' he sneered.

The leopard was very much bigger than Gargoyle, and seemed to have no manners at all. Gargoyle sat up in a dignified manner and casually licked a paw.

'That's all right,' said Gargoyle, condescendingly. 'Take it, if you think it's worth the trouble.' (The young animal had by now scuttled off into the bush.) 'I don't have to do this for a living. I'm just here for the sport.'

'You smell of men,' sneered the leopard. 'Alley cat!' And with one bound he disappeared into the jungle.

Gargoyle sat tidying his whiskers, pretending to be quite calm, but really his feelings were deeply hurt and his nerves badly upset. The leopard had made him feel small. He had been the Primitive Hunter before, part of the jungle, an animal living to the full. Rather childish, he told himself now. He was, of course, a Civilized Cat, with men to work for him and give him milk. He thought he'd had enough of the jungle.

To his ears came a sound that was not of the jungle, a thumping, a throbbing, that Gargoyle at first thought was some sort of machine. It was certainly something made by man and Gargoyle was glad to hear it. Out of the clearing ran a path that seemed to lead towards the sound and he set off along it.

Now that he was a Civilized Cat the smells, sound and shadowy shapes of the jungle made him nervous instead of exciting him. His heart fluttered with alarm at a rustle in a thicket, the shriek of a bird sent an icy shiver down his spine, and he kept looking backwards over his shoulder. He began to learn what it felt like to be hunted, instead of hunting.

Through the trees at the far end of the dark tunnel of jungle track, there was a flicker of red light. That meant fire, and fire meant Man. His ears laid back, Gargoyle bolted out of the jungle as if every creature that roared, shrieked and rustled were on his track and hunting him down.

Gargoyle strolled into the open space between a cluster of thatched beehive huts. The firelight flickered on black bodies daubed with strange designs in white clay, squatting round in a large circle.

A band of drummers beat out a rhythm on the skins of their drums:

BOOMPadoopa BOOMPadoopa BOOMPadoopa

A group of men with white-streaked faces and long thin black legs went dreamily round to the rhythm of the drums, kicking up the dust with their stamping, shuffling feet:

BOOMPadoopa BOOMPadoopa BOOMPadoopa
STAMPshuffle STAMPshuffle STAMPshuffle

Gargoyle sat down next to a white cockerel who seemed to be deeply interested too, and watched and listened. The squatting circle joined in with hand-claps:

BOOMPadoopa BOOMPadoopa BOOMPadoopa
STAMPshuffle STAMPshuffle STAMPshuffle
CLAP CLAP CLAP

Gargoyle stared without blinking. He had never seen this sort of thing in Ramsly, except perhaps at Youth Club dances, which he had often sniffed at and passed by. His heart, after pounding with the excitement of the hunt, and fluttering with the fear of being hunted, now settled down and thumped to this fierce rhythm:

BOOMPadoopa BOOMPadoopa BOOMPadoopa
(*the drums*)
STAMPshuffle STAMPshuffle STAMPshuffle
(*the dancers*)
CLAP CLAP CLAP
(*the hands*)
aTHUMP aTHUMP aTHUMP
(*Gargoyle's heart*)

Gargoyle's heart gave an additional thump as into the firelight leapt the most hideous figure he had ever seen. The face was as big as a man's body, with great narrow cat's eyes and a crooked mouth full of broken teeth. Round the Face was a bush of straggling grassy hair, beneath it were what looked like a man's legs, shaggy at the knees with more straw hair, and out of its ears came two manlike arms, one hand holding a short sharp spear and the other a rattle made of bones.

The thing leapt and twisted among the dancers and shook its rattle:

BOOMPadoopa BOOMPadoopa BOOMPadoopa
STAMPshuffle STAMPshuffle STAMPshuffle
CLAP CLAP CLAP
aTHUMP aTHUMP aTHUMP
RATTLErattle RATTLErattle RATTLErattle
(*the bones*)

The Face whirled among the dancers threatening them with the spear and the bones, and the dancers were now more and more excited as they threw themselves about in movements telling of fear, begging for mercy, seeking for escape. The rhythm grew faster and faster, the sounds more and more mixed up:

BOOMPadoopa BOOMPadoopa BOOMPadoopa
STAMPshuffle STAMPshuffle STAMPshuffle
rattle CLAP rattle CLAP rattle CLAP rattle CLAP rattle
BOOMPshuffleBOOMPshuffleBOOMPshuffleBOOMPshu
STAMPCLAP STAMPCLAP STAMPCLAP
BOOMPshufflethumpSTAMPCLAPthumpSTAMPrattle
BOOMPadoopaSTAMPCLAPRATTLEshuffleBOOMsh

In the base of Gargoyle's spine the nerves twitched in time to the rhythm, and he lashed his tail just as the dancers waggled their grass skirts.

BOOMPadoopaSTAMPCLAPRATTLEshuffleBOOMsh
Wagglewagglewagglewagglewagglewagglewagglewagglewaggle

Gargoyle felt himself part of the dance, the rhythm, the handclaps, the heat, the dust and the flickering firelight. He belonged to the black-legged dancers, the white-painted handclappers, the drummers, even to the

fearful creature with the great cat's eyes. They could do what they liked with him. He was theirs.

The great Face with legs advanced leaping towards Gargoyle and the white cockerel, who sat fascinated as it came towards them. Gargoyle let himself be picked up by the human hand coming from the side of the Face. In the other hand the short sharp spear was raised, shining in the firelight.

(The shaggy hair round the Face was like the raffia the old ladies of Church Square used for making mats.)

And as soon as Gargoyle thought of the old ladies of Church Square the spell was broken. The Face was only a wooden mask fringed with raffia, worn by a dancing African. But the short sharp spear was real.

Gargoyle bit the witch-doctor smartly in the right thumb, dropped to the ground, and then bolted between the legs of the dancers and up the side of a thatched hut.

The white cockerel, also released from the spell, flapped wildly into the air and joined him on the roof of the hut. The drumming and dancing stopped and there was a babble of voices, some laughing, some angry. The rapt dancers and drummers had become a confused crowd of African villagers, but some of them were seizing up stones, sticks and light spears to throw at Gargoyle who had spoiled their ceremony. At that moment there was a great flash of blue lightning, an appalling explosion of thunder right overhead, and rain came pouring down like a waterfall.

'Get us out of here!' spat Gargoyle at the cockerel, showing his teeth. 'Which way to the sea?'

'But I live here!' cackled the cockerel foolishly. 'They need me.'

'I bet they do!' snapped Gargoyle, taking him by the throat. 'Which way to the sea? The Big Water?'

Choking, the cockerel pointed with his beak through the trees, and as sticks and stones came whizzing through the air, hurled by those members of the crowd who were not put off by the drenching rain, Gargoyle let go of the cockerel, sprang from the top of the hut to a branch of a forest tree, and made off as fast as he could go from branch to branch and from tree to tree. Soon the young men who were hunting him gave up the chase, and it was not very long before, in a flash of lightning, he saw through the branches a stretch of turbulent water.

But it was not the sea. It was a great river. And as Gargoyle clung to the branches threshing in the wind, the storm water undermined the roots of his tree and

the storm wind blew it with a crash and splash into the swollen river.

'Why,' Gargoyle asked himself, 'did I ever leave home?' He was sitting in the branch of a tree. All right, he had sat in branches of trees before. He was alone – but he didn't mind being alone. All around him was the bright blue sparkling sea, and he had to admit that it looked very cheerful.

What he did not like, and had never tried before, was sitting all alone in the branch of a tree in the middle of the sea.

The tree he was sitting in had floated down the river and been carried by the force of the current right away from the coast. So there he was, and as there was nothing he could do about it and the storm had died down, he curled himself up in the fork of the branches and went to sleep.

6. In the Far Southern Seas

GARGOYLE woke from his sleep shivering and mewing. So he sat up on the branch and washed his face, and felt better, and as he was doing so he saw, floating in the mirror-like sea, the town of Ramsly. The same current that had swept him down the river and out to sea had carried the town away from the coast once more.

The currents that creep along the beds of the deep oceans are curious things. They take no notice of the winds and currents on the surface of the sea, but move along in their own good time between pole and pole, or East and West around the great continents. One of these deep drifts had once again got hold of the base of the floating town and was driving it steadily through the still upper layers of the water. Like a majestic ship Ramsly bore very slowly but surely down upon Gargoyle's forest tree, and as it rubbed along the Fishmarket he jumped easily ashore.

Ramsly continued on its way through the tropical seas. Day followed day, week followed week, and the people who were left in the town carried on a dream-like way of life, no longer caring where they were going or what was to become of them. Nobody cared that no electricity or water came into the houses. They sat among the young coconut palms in the churchyard, under the brilliant tropical moon and stars, and prepared simple meals from the food they accepted as gifts from visiting ships, and they drew water from the old town well which the tropical storms kept refilling. By day they sat and watched the long blue ocean swells pass by; almost big enough, they seemed, to give the whole mass of the town a slow, sleepy, gentle rocking motion. In the up-currents of air caused by the westerly trade winds blowing against the church, the great albatrosses floated and circled on their six-foot wings. Gargoyle noticed their heavy, hooked yellow beaks when they settled on the church tower and he was most polite to them. The young people who were left still fished all day from points round the edge of the town, until they got tired of pulling ashore strange fish. Indeed, flying fish often landed themselves almost in the very frying-pans of the people who lived in the Fishmarket. But nobody now bathed; apart from the danger of being left behind forever in the middle of the ocean, there were too many sharks cruising curiously around.

The people who were not happy unless they were making more money, improving things, or getting famous, had now left Ramsly, or if they hadn't they were now leaving on any ship that would take them off. The old ladies of Church Square, who had always really decided the things that mattered in Ramsly, were now left in open control of the town. Chief among them, or rather Queen among them, was Miss Fitzbuller. In spite of salty sea winds, tropical damp, or blowing dust, her silver teapot had always been polished, her lace tablecloths washed and starched, and her mahogany furniture gleaming. She and a devoted old servant kept her house fresh and spotless, and always ready for her to entertain her friends with tea and conversation. The last of the Ramsly magistrates, she held court at the Town Hall whenever there were quarrels to settle.

So long had they been at sea, with no sight of land – so much longer than any ship ever invented had stayed at sea – that everyone had *almost* decided that Ramsly was going to be an island in the South Indian Ocean for the rest of time. The only thing that made them doubt was the behaviour of the clocks – or was it the behaviour of the sun? Up to now the clocks that had been wound for generations in the sitting-rooms of Ramsly had continued to tell their owners more or less the time to get up, take their midday meal, and go to bed. Now everyone was complaining of their clocks running slow. Every time a ship called, which was not so often now, the Captain would give Miss Fitzbuller a point on the map which was a little further East. Every month, Miss Fitzbuller would call a meeting at the Town Hall to decide what time it was. There wasn't much else to worry about.

One calm clear night, when for once the steady trade wind had dropped and puffs of breeze blew gently from various directions, Gargoyle, who was sitting on the church tower from habit, once again smelt land. Now the smell of land from the sea is like what landsmen call the smell of the sea from inland. It is the smell of the beach really, of seaweed and empty crab shells. What made Gargoyle sure it was a new smell was that, mixed with it, came a whiff of spices, unlike anything that grew in the churchyard. Gargoyle's midnight restlessness, which had slept for months, awoke in him again. He wandered down to Miss Fitzbuller's house, and up to her bedroom, where she was reading *Pride and Prejudice* by the light of a candle for the twenty-third time. (She found the books left by passing ships mostly uninteresting.)

'What's the matter, Gargoyle?' asked Miss Fitzbuller. 'How restless you are tonight!'

At daybreak Gargoyle was up on the tower again, sniffing the air and looking around. Sure enough, there on the eastern horizon was a low dark shape that might have been a cloud. All that day it hovered on the edge of the sea, and at noon a solitary thundercloud, alone in the light blue sky, formed over the island, alone in the dark blue sea. But nothing happened that day, though at night the teasing breaths of spice came over the waters.

The next day the wind blew steadily again, and tacking against it came a graceful boat with white sails. It tied up at the quay and a handsome dark bronze man, wearing a short-sleeved shirt and a cotton kilt, jumped ashore with an important-looking letter. He was directed as a matter of course to Miss Fitzbuller's house, where he presented it with a polite salute to the old servant and squatted down on the doorstep to wait, like a statue set to guard the door.

Miss Fitzbuller sat on her mahogany settee, upholstered in red-striped satin, adjusted her spectacles, and opened the letter.

'Well, well!' murmured Miss Fitzbuller to Gargoyle. 'Just fancy! A letter from a dear old school-friend.' She moved over to her tidy bureau to write an answer. Gargoyle sniffed inquisitively at the strange letter. It smelt of spice.

Miss Fitzbuller handed her letter, in a neat blue envelope, to the bronze statue at the door, gave him a charming smile and got a polite salute and a flash of strong white teeth in return, and the strange seaman was away down the cobbled street in his bare feet. As he leapt from the quay to the waiting boat, nobody noticed that Gargoyle had followed him on board. He hadn't waited for an invitation this time.

With a fair wind, the little boat flew over the sea towards the distant island, and after an hour or so it came alongside a jetty built out from a sandy shore. Soon Gargoyle was on land again, and nosing around

among the coconut palms, the low, airy buildings, the goats and chickens and little black pigs, and the happy playing children.

This place, Gargoyle felt, was a place where a cat could live as a cat should. He rolled luxuriously in the white shelly sand, he sharpened his claws and stretched himself against the palm tree trunks, he sniffed the smells of living things, growing things, and spice. The people, too, seemed to be remarkably active and interested in food. As the day went on there were more and more men, women and children carrying baskets of fruit, landing nets full of fish, chopping roots, lighting cooking fires. All the food seemed to be collecting in a clearing near one long low building with a flagpole outside it. Flocks of goats were driven up to be milked, and nobody seemed to mind Gargoyle helping himself.

All night the preparing of food went on, and all next day. In the morning a big sailing sloop set sail in the direction of Ramsly and in the evening, amid much excitement, she was sighted returning to harbour, and down to the jetty to meet her came a group of dignified dark-skinned men in jackets and cotton kilts, and with them a tall stately lady in a long white dress. This was the Queen of Sunday Island.

As the sloop made fast alongside the jetty, Gargoyle saw that Miss Fitzbuller was on the deck. She stepped ashore and she and the Queen of Sunday Island embraced each other.

'My dear Lottie,' said Miss Fitzbuller. 'How wonderful to see you again. It must be forty years since we were at school together.'

The two ladies walked together under the palms towards the building with the flag outside it, talking of hockey teams and school chums.

'My dear!' exclaimed Miss Fitzbuller, noticing the piles of pineapples, roast pigs, shellfish, and puddings baked in leaves, all spread out under the trees. 'What a lot of *food!* Is it somebody's birthday?'

The Queen smilingly said that it was indeed her birthday, and she was very glad to have her old schoolfriend as guest of honour. And as the sun went down in a great red sunset over the western sea, and the huge tropical moon rose over the palm trees to the East, the people of Sunday Island and their guest sat down to eat and drink, and musicians played their stringed instruments, and singers sang their plaintive songs and a group of girls danced a graceful dance.

While everyone was at his happiest, Gargoyle pricked his ears, for he heard a sound that did not belong. It was the sound of a motor-boat making for the jetty. It stopped, and after a while two figures strode into the circle of firelight. One of them was tall, in an immaculate white suit that made him seem taller still, with a sword at his waist and a lot of gold about the shoulders and cap. The other was shorter and burlier, in a white suit of a different shape and a blue sailor collar. Gargoyle recognized him at once. It was Able Seaman Sippers. And the tall one was the Captain of the *Incredible.*

There was a dead silence as the Captain walked up to where the Queen was sitting on her throne of carved wood decorated with sharks' teeth. He halted in front of her, saluted stiffly and bowed. The Queen said not a word but looked at him questioningly.

'Your Majesty – ' said the Captain, and then stopped and swallowed. He cleared his throat and began again.

'Your Majesty – ' but again he choked and could say nothing more.

Miss Fitzbuller, looking round in bewilderment, saw that two tears were running down the Queen's cheeks. She looked at the grave councillors, at the musicians, at the dancing girls standing like statues, at all the islanders sitting round on the feasting ground. All of them were motionless, and every face was streaming with tears. Miss Fitzbuller broke the silence.

'My dear Lottie,' she asked quietly. 'Whatever is the matter?'

The Queen turned to Miss Fitzbuller, and did not try to hide her tears.

'The Captain has come to tell us that we must leave the island. They are going to make a big explosion and it will not be safe here. We have been expecting this, but it still makes us very sad.'

There was a pause, during which Gargoyle and Able

Seaman Sippers glared at each other on the edge of the crowd.

'Is this true, Captain?' asked Miss Fitzbuller.

The Captain drove the end of his scabbard fiercely into the soft sand, and looked at his feet.

'Madam, I wish with all my heart that it were not true. I've done what I can for the people of Sunday Island, and of course we'll look after them. But a Deuteronium bomb is to be exploded in this area and it's my job to evacuate this island.'

Miss Fitzbuller thought for a moment.

'Captain,' she said, 'I don't know about these things. How long would a wireless message take to get to London?'

'An hour or so. But it's too late, I've been sending them for weeks. I've thought of everything.'

'There's something which you probably have not thought of. You will kindly make a signal (I think that's the correct expression) to the Prime Minister of England, informing him that the Free and Ancient Borough of Ramsly is now in the target area and he'll have to set off his bomb somewhere else. And you can sign it Aunt Adelaide.'

This time the Captain really did choke. They revived him with palm wine and sago pudding, and after he had satisfied himself that Miss Fitzbuller really was the Prime Minister's aunt, he called for Able Seaman Sippers, who fetched a signalman from the motor-boat, who flashed a signal to the *Incredible* at anchor offshore, from where it went by radio to Australia, and from there by urgent secret priority cable to London, where the Prime Minister, just as he was putting on his hat to go to the House of Commons, was handed the message on a piece of paper and said: 'Oh my *Aunt!*'

So the Prime Minister of Great Britain started another worrying day, but on Sunday Island they were already coming to the end of that very same day, and they had quite forgotten their worries. The Captain ordered immediate shore leave for the Starboard Watch, so that half the ship's company joined the feast. The sailors danced with the island girls, and Able Seaman Sippers did a comic dance all by himself, and the Captain and Miss Adelaide Fitzbuller were so loaded with garlands by the happy islanders that the Captain said he felt like the First Prize at the village Flower Show. Even Gargoyle was treated as a hero: like the sailors, he was fed with tidbits and had his head stroked by a dark-eyed dusky maiden – one of the younger ones, about three years old.

There was so much food that the feast went on for the best part of a week, as was usual on Sunday Island, so that everybody from Ramsly and the *Incredible* took it in turn for a run ashore on the island. One of the youngest sailors was even heard to say that Singapore and Sydney were all right, but this was as good as a picnic back home with grandma and auntie and all.

But after the best part of a very good week the *Incredible* weighed anchor and steamed away. In the meanwhile Ramsly had been drifting past the island and further and further to the East, and it took longer and longer for the sailing boats to return from the town to the island. At last the time came when Miss Fitzbuller had to decide that it would be the last trip of the sailing schooner between Ramsly and Sunday.

The voyage now took all day, so the Queen was to sail to Ramsly and spend the night at Miss Fitzbuller's comfortable house in Church Square, and to set off back to the island at first light next day.

That night the Queen and Miss Fitzbuller talked of

old times and looked at old faded photographs, and the other ladies of Church Square called in to say good-bye to Her Majesty. When the time came for them to go to bed Miss Fitzbuller and the other old ladies thought of the happy life on Sunday Island with its schools, and its church, and its wise old men to manage things and its strong young men to do things, and then they thought of Ramsly drifting, perhaps forever, about the oceans of the world. And instead of going to bed the ladies of Church Square spent the night packing their clothes and their treasures. At first light next morning the crew of the schooner loaded the hold and the decks with cabin trunks and hatboxes, and the ladies of Church Square, some of them in tears, trooped over the gangway on to the ship. As they did so, Gargoyle sat alone on the quay. One of the crew went with a grin to pick him up, but Miss Fitzbuller, from the deck, stopped him with a gesture. Gargoyle turned his back on the ship and walked slowly towards the West Cliff steps.

There was a flat calm as the mooring ropes were let go, and it was the town that could be felt moving steadily eastward, leaving the ship standing idle in the middle of the ocean.

And so, as the sun rose above the chimney-stacks of Ramsly, and the quayside moved further and further from the ship, this quaint old-world town, this bit of old England, said farewell to these romantic Southern seas, this tropical paradise, this gracious Island Queen, and carried with it happy memories of its visit.

7. Waltzing Matilda

THE swagman sat beside the billabong, waiting. He was dressed in a bush hat and a bush jacket and tattered khaki trousers. His face was black and his legs were long and thin, and he had woolly hair and a woolly beard. He was a swagman because he carried all his belongings in a bundle, and he was going for a walk of a thousand miles or so, and he sat beside a billabong because that was the kind of country it was, mostly red dust and rock, with his billabong, a nearly dried-up watercourse, cutting through it. He was waiting for a handful of large white witchetty grubs to finish cooking in the ashes of a fire, so that he could have his supper. And just then along came a black-and-white animal he had never seen before, and sat down beside him.

Joe (that was the swagman's name) was very much surprised. If there was one thing he thought he knew all about it was animals. His ancestors had hunted animals over these red dusty plains for thousands of years. He himself had been born on these plains and had learnt about wild animals from his tribe, but he had also worked with the white men and learnt about sheep and cattle, and how to shoe horses, and even to drive a car, but he had got a bit bored with it all and decided to go for a walk-about. He was quite happy looking after himself in the bush because he knew how to dig for grubs and roots, and he knew the habits of all the animals. But here was a black-and-white animal he had never even seen.

'Hallo,' said Joe. 'What are you?' He spoke in a language that animals can understand – the aborigines of Australia are among the few people in the world who can do this.

'I'm a cat,' replied Gargoyle, rather contemptuously.

Joe remembered a book he had read. C, A, T, had been one of the first words in it. 'Cat,' his teacher had said. It hadn't meant anything to Joe at the time, so that was about as far as he had got with books. Now, lo and behold, here was a cat. Joe thought there might be something in books after all.

'What you doing here, cat?' asked Joe.

'Going for a walk,' said Gargoyle.

'Me too,' said Joe. He stirred his grubs in the ashes.

'Is that all there is to eat on this island?' he asked.

'Very big land. Plenty to eat,' grunted Joe.

'I don't eat grubs,' said Gargoyle.

'No? You go catch something big then!' Joe laughed.

Gargoyle got cross. 'I've just been hunting some of your animals. I was stalking a thing like a big rat or a long-legged rabbit. What do you think it did? Went and jumped into the pocket of another animal like itself only much bigger, and it went bouncing away on its hind legs. Is that a proper way for an animal to behave?'

Joe laughed a lot at this.

'Where you come from, cat, that you don't know about kangaroos and I don't know about you? You dropped from the skies?'

'I'm from Ramsly, of course,' sniffed Gargoyle. Joe looked blank.

'Where's that?' he asked. Gargoyle pointed just over the sandhills.

'Nothing there but the sea,' said Joe. 'You don't look like a fish.'

'Where do you come from,' said Gargoyle, 'that you don't know about the floating Borough of Ramsly? Come and see for yourself.'

But Joe's grubs were ready to eat now, and he dug them with a twig out of the hot sand and ashes and dusted them. He offered one to Gargoyle and crunched the others. Gargoyle turned up his nose at first, but he was very hungry so he took a bite. To his surprise it tasted like roast pork. He could have done with some more.

After their supper Gargoyle led Joe to where Ramsly had fetched up against the barren North-west coast of Australia. Between the endless dusty red plains to the East and the boundless ocean to the West, washed with red watercolour by the setting sun, the town looked more forlorn and lost than it had ever been. Was this the end of its journey, and was this wild desert man the only one to welcome its arrival?

As Joe stalked wonderingly up the cobbled streets, what was left of Ramsly's population looked anxiously out of their windows at this strange figure with woolly hair, wrinkled black face, and hunter's stride.

What was left of Ramsly's population were the real Ramslyers, descendants of the families who had lived there since the town had been a haunt of fierce seamen and wild marsh-dwellers. Samuel Fazzick looked out from his antique shop, nervously fingering a flintlock gun. Theodore Horsa, the only true Ramsly artist, roused himself as he saw Joe and reached for a sketchbook. Old Mrs Guffle peeped through her lace curtains.

'Remember Cousin Colin what went to Australia?' whispered Mrs Guffle to her even older mother. 'If that's him, he hasn't half changed.'

Joe followed Gargoyle through the churchyard. In the other direction, through the gravestones, came old Ezekiel Lamb, the only person in the world who carried the whole past history of Ramsly in his head. He was over ninety, and he had not noticed anything new in Ramsly for thirty years. He did not notice Joe, but walked past looking into nothing.

Joe shivered. 'Plenty ghosts here,' he said to himself. He came to a bench where three silent old men were sitting. He sat down beside them. They grunted. Joe grunted. All four went on sitting in silence.

*

Weeks passed, and Ramsly was still stuck to the barren North-west coast of Australia, cut off from the rest of the country by the waterless desert. More black tribesmen, wandering along the coast alone or in families, came to gape at the deserted streets, and, when they found that nobody minded, moved into the empty houses. Pearl fishers, sponge-fishers, shark-fishers of many races and colours called from time to time in their sea-going vessels. Smugglers of one kind and another used Ramsly as their headquarters. And worse than smugglers. It was like old times for Ramsly – the very old times.

One moonless night Gargoyle picked his way up Mermaid Street. A babble of oaths and argument came from the Mermaid Inn, then the sounds of tables being overturned and glasses breaking. A bottle came hurtling through one of the windows and splintered on the cobbles. Gargoyle hid behind a barrel in the middle of the street as a man came running out of the Mermaid, followed by a figure with a knife that gleamed in the lamplight. Two pairs of running footsteps echoed down the steep street to the Strand, then there was a scream and a splash, and something like silence returned to Mermaid Street. There was only a woman's voice wailing a strange Eastern chant from Elder House, and the rattle of dice from the opium den in Mermaid Cottage.

Gargoyle was used to such goings on in Ramsly now, but he had taken to living in the church tower, more to keep out of the way of rough seaboots and flying bottles than in the hope of seeing anything. But tonight as he gazed around at the velvet sky shining with great stars and the inky sea lit with splashes of phosphorescence, there *was* something.

Above the sound of the sea came the faint beat of powerful engines. Dimly, to the south-west, Gargoyle could see the outline of two long low motor-ships creeping towards the Fishmarket Quay. The engines cut

out, the two vessels came efficiently alongside, and Gargoyle heard orders muttered quietly as uniformed men jumped over the side and formed up on the quay.

Then there was a cry of alarm from one of the old houses, and a shot. The shot was answered by a rattle of fire from a light automatic gun; there were more confused cries, more single shots, and then it seemed that a running battle was beginning all up and down the cobbled streets, in and out of the hidden passages and alleyways, over the jumbled roofs and even from cellar to cellar of the oldest houses. The engines of the strange craft lying along the other side of the town were started up and the sounds of firing, shouting and running footsteps moved towards them. One after another, amid cries and curses in several languages, the vessels of the fishers, smugglers and pirates put to sea, and quiet returned to the streets of the town.

Gargoyle came down from the tower to see what was happening now. A big bearded officer in uniform was going from door to door, accompanied by sailors in shorts, carrying automatic rifles at the ready. Gargoyle walked up to the officer and rubbed himself against his stockings, just to show he was on the right side.

' 'Allo, Puss,' said the officer. 'You're a beaut, aren't you. We've cleared out that lot of no-good pirates. Now you can show me where the old folks at home are.'

They went from door to door, Gargoyle leading the way and mewing outside the houses where he expected to find the remaining Ramslyers. But they found nobody.

Next day the Australian sailors searched the town again in daylight, but not a human being did they find. Somewhere, among the many races that come and go over the Eastern Indian Ocean, the Timor Sea, and among the islands, the last families of Ramsly had disappeared.

The bearded officer sat on a barrel with a glass in his hand, thinking.

'You know, we're short of houses in Australia, moggie,' he said to Gargoyle. 'It's a shame to see a whole town going begging. The old place is a bit crooked looking but she's better than nothing. If she floats on the next spring tide I'll send some tugs and get her towed down to Fremantle.'

At the next spring tide Ramsly did float. With a fleet of powerful ocean-going tugs churning away at the ends of massive hurricane hawsers, the town moved southwards down the coast. There was plenty of time for all the important people of Perth, the capital of Western Australia, and Fremantle, its port, to prepare a grand civic welcome to the first bit of the Old Country to float halfway round the world. There were to be bands, and fireworks, and watersports, and of course a cricket match. People flew from all over the continent to see this great event, but to represent the freemen, tax-payers and property-holders of Ramsly there was only Gargoyle, the cat.

As Ramsly reached the latitude of Fremantle, scores of sailing yachts, launches and steamers carrying brass bands came out to meet it. The order was given to the tugs to alter course to port so as to bring the town in to the shore. With much churning of screws the tugs came round so that the tow lines led towards the land. The bands struck up 'Waltzing Matilda' and 'A Life on the Ocean Wave', the sirens hooted and the people cheered.

Ramsly went drifting South.

The big tugs exerted their full power, and thrashed the blue water into white suds. Smaller tugs bustled out from the harbour and nuzzled against the flank of the town. Even the big steamers, crowded with sightseers, got out tow lines and added their weight, but apart from pulling up a few lamp-posts they seemed to make no difference. Ramsly went serenely on, towards the South.

Australians are not people who give up quickly once they have started something. It was decided that if the course of the town could not be altered, it must be anchored where it was. Every spare anchor from the shipyards, antique kedges from forgotten clippers, enormous bower anchors for modern liners, great blocks of concrete for mooring buoys, were ferried out from the docks, with every available link of heavy cable. But the trouble was what to make them fast to. If they put a wire rope round a house, the whole building was pulled slowly and sadly into the sea. Working like demons, the gangs of sailors and dockyard maties at last got a strop of the thickest wire hawsers, shackled end to end, right round the entire town, and to this they secured as many anchors and cables as they could, and let them go to the sea bed at once.

The cables and hawsers slowly took the strain. Everyone held his breath and watched. Then, with a twang that could be heard on the distant shore, the hawser parted, men leapt wildly to escape the wire that writhed like a sea serpent round the town and the whole of the gear slipped irresistibly into the sea.

The sun was setting. The exhausted men were taken off the floating town, the pleasure steamers and sailing yachts went home. The fireworks were cancelled, and rain stopped the cricket match.

'If she won't stay, let the old borough go!' said the Australians.

Beyond the farthest point inhabited by man, the town was moving South still. Deep down below the surface of the sea, the unknown current was bearing against the bottom of the floating rock and driving it towards the long Antarctic night. The albatrosses deserted the churchyard, and as the ice floes thickened around the quaysides the penguins took over. More sedate than any visitors that Ramsly had ever known, they toddled in their neat black-and-white suits up and down the cobbled streets, peered with polite interest into the bow windows, still showing notices like 'Home-made fudge' and 'Hand-woven tweed', and sat in silence on the church pews.

There was only one thing to disturb their peace: a fiend that was black-and-white like themselves, a cold, lonely, hungry spirit that lurked in attics and cellars, and stole scraps of fish brought ashore by the penguins, and even lay in wait for the smaller birds to attack them with claws and teeth. It was the last living creature left after Ramsly's long voyage – Gargoyle, the rectory cat, who had evaded every attempt to take him away from his old haunts, and now was left alone among the crowds of suspicious penguins, to represent the artists, the retired gentlefolk, the public servants, the old families, and the ordinary people of Ramsly.

Now the snow began to pile higher and higher over the cobbles and against the old brick walls, a snow that would never melt. As the weight of more snow pressed upon the first layers, the streets and houses became encased in solid ice. At last, frozen immovably into the great Southern ice-cap, the ancient English Borough of Ramsly reached the end of its journey, preserved forever beneath a smooth white mound.

And Gargoyle? Well, captains go down with their ships and cats stick to their old homes, but cats have nine lives too. And Gargoyle, after all, became quite a famous cat.

There were a lot of expeditions to the South Pole that year. On one of the new maps they made of the Polar regions there is a new landmark: 'Steeple Rock'. The explorer who first noticed this lonely ice hill thought that the black rock sticking out of the top looked like the tip of a church steeple.

It was. Living inside the tip of Ramsly church steeple was Gargoyle. Through a broken slate he looked out at a white world to the South, ice and a lead-coloured sea to the North. A pale sun circled round the horizon and never set. Gargoyle sat and waited for the night.

He was cold. Too cold to remember clearly the nights in farmyards, nights under the desert stars, jungle nights, tropical island nights, nights of storm and nights of wild adventure. He only knew that his was a land where night never seemed to come. It was no place for a cat.

Something moved on the white plain below. A kind

of serpent with many legs snaking over the snow? No, a string of animals – dogs harnessed together, pulling a sledge with a man on it. And another line of dogs, and another. As Gargoyle watched, the dog teams halted, the men unpacked the sledges and put up a little tent. They tethered the dogs and threw food to them and then disappeared into the tent.

Gargoyle crept out on to the snow and painfully made his way down the slope towards the camp. The dogs set up a furious yelping, but something about Gargoyle's frozen green stare made them quieten down.

'Hallo, you dogs!' said Gargoyle. 'Where are *you* going?'

'South,' barked the leading dog. 'Where else?'

'Where else indeed?' said Gargoyle. 'I've been going South for ages. I and my town.'

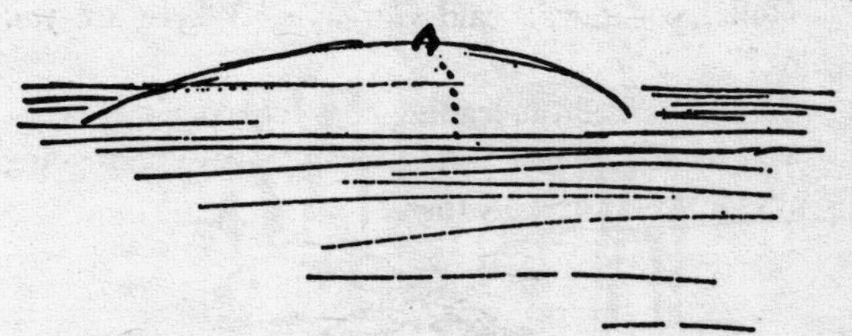

He crept in through a kind of sleeve that was the entrance to the tent. Three hairy, bearded men sat there, frozen like statues in the act of drinking hot cocoa – but frozen only with surprise at seeing a black-and-white cat walk in from nowhere.

'Hallo!' said Gargoyle. 'You've been a long time coming to take me away! Got any milk?'

You probably remember the picture in the newspapers: 'First Cat to Reach South Pole.' There was nothing remarkable about men at the Pole that year, and of course dogs were two a penny. But nobody could make out exactly where that cat had come from.

The End

Also by Clive King

STIG OF THE DUMP

Barney is a solitary eight-year-old, given to wandering off by himself. One day he is lying on the edge of a disused chalk pit when he tumbles over, lands in a sort of cave and meets 'somebody with a lot of shaggy hair and two bright black eyes' – wearing a rabbit skin and speaking in grunts. He names him Stig, they learn to understand each other, and together they raid the rubbish dump at the bottom of the pit, improve Stig's cave dwelling, and enjoy a series of adventures that are sometimes wildly improbable and sometimes extremely realistic.

ME AND MY MILLION

When his older brother asked him to deliver a bag of laundry, Ringo had a fair idea what would be in it. But he hadn't reckoned on getting lost and finding himself in a strange neighbourhood with a picture worth a million pounds!

THE TWENTY-TWO LETTERS

'Look, your Majesty, even you could read it in a few minutes if I showed you. Only twenty-two letters!' Beth doesn't know that she's describing the invention of the alphabet or that she's living at a time when civilization is taking several huge steps forward. And that's just the beginning of this dramatic and exciting story.

COME BACK SOON

Judy Gardiner

Val's family seem quite an odd bunch, and their life is hectic but happy. But then Val's mother walks out on them and Val's carefree life is suddenly quite different. This is a moving but funny story.

AMY'S EYES

Richard Kennedy

When a doll changes into a man it means that anything might happen . . . and in this magical story all kinds of strange and wonderful things do happen to Amy and her sailor doll, the Captain. Together they set off on a fantastic journey on a quest for treasure more valuable than mere gold.

ASTERCOTE

Penelope Lively

Astercote village was destroyed by plague in the fourteenth century, and Mair and her brother Peter find themselves caught up in a strange adventure when an ancient superstition is resurrected.

THE HOUNDS OF THE MÓRRÍGAN

Pat O'Shea

When the Great Queen Mórrígan, evil creature from the world of Irish mythology, returns to destroy the world, Pidge and Brigit are the children chosen to thwart her. How they go about it makes a hilarious, moving story, full of totally original and unforgettable characters.

JELLYBEAN

Tessa Duder

A sensitive modern novel about Geraldine, alias 'Jellybean', who leads a rather solitary life as the only child of a single parent. She's tired of having to fit in with her mother's busy schedule, but a new friend and a performance of 'The Nutcracker Suite' change everything.

THE PRIESTS OF FERRIS

Maurice Gee

Susan Ferris and her cousin Nick return to the world of O which they had saved from the evil Halfmen, only to find that O is now ruled by cruel and ruthless priests. Can they save the inhabitants of O from tyranny? An action-packed and gripping story by the author of prize-winning *The Halfmen of O*.

THE SEA IS SINGING

Rosalind Kerven

In her Shetland home, Tess is torn between the plight of the whales and loyalty to her father and his job on the oil rig. A haunting and thought-provoking novel.

BACK HOME

Michelle Magorian

A marvellously gripping story of an irrepressible girl's struggle to adjust to a new life. Twelve-year-old Rusty, who had been evacuated to the United States when she was seven, returns to the grey austerity of post-war Britain.

THE BEAST MASTER

Andre Norton

Spine-chilling science fiction – treachery and revenge! Hosteen Storm is a man with a mission to find and punish Brad Quade, the man who killed his father long ago on Terra, the planet where life no longer exists.

WOOF!

Allan Ahlberg

Eric had always wanted a dog, so he was not unhappy when he found he had turned into a dog one night – especially when he found he could change back again! Fritz Wegner's drawings illustrate this funny and exciting story superbly.

VERA PRATT AND THE FALSE MOUSTACHES

Brough Girling

There were times when Wally Pratt wished his mum was more ordinary and not the fanatic mechanic she was, but when he and his friends find themselves caught up in a real 'cops and robbers' affair, he is more than glad to have his mum, Vera, to help them.

SADDLEBOTTOM

Dick King-Smith

Hilarious adventures of a Wessex Saddleback pig whose white saddle is in the wrong place, to the chagrin of his mother.

SLADE

John Tully

Slade has a mission – to investigate life on Earth. When Eddie discovers the truth about Slade he gets a whole lot more adventure than he bargained for.

A TASTE OF BLACKBERRIES

Doris Buchanan Smith

The moving story about a young boy who has to come to terms with the tragic death of his best friend and the guilty feeling that he could somehow have saved him.